Howling Hill

by
WILL HOBBS

illustrated by
JILL KASTNER

Morrow Junior Books
NEW YORK

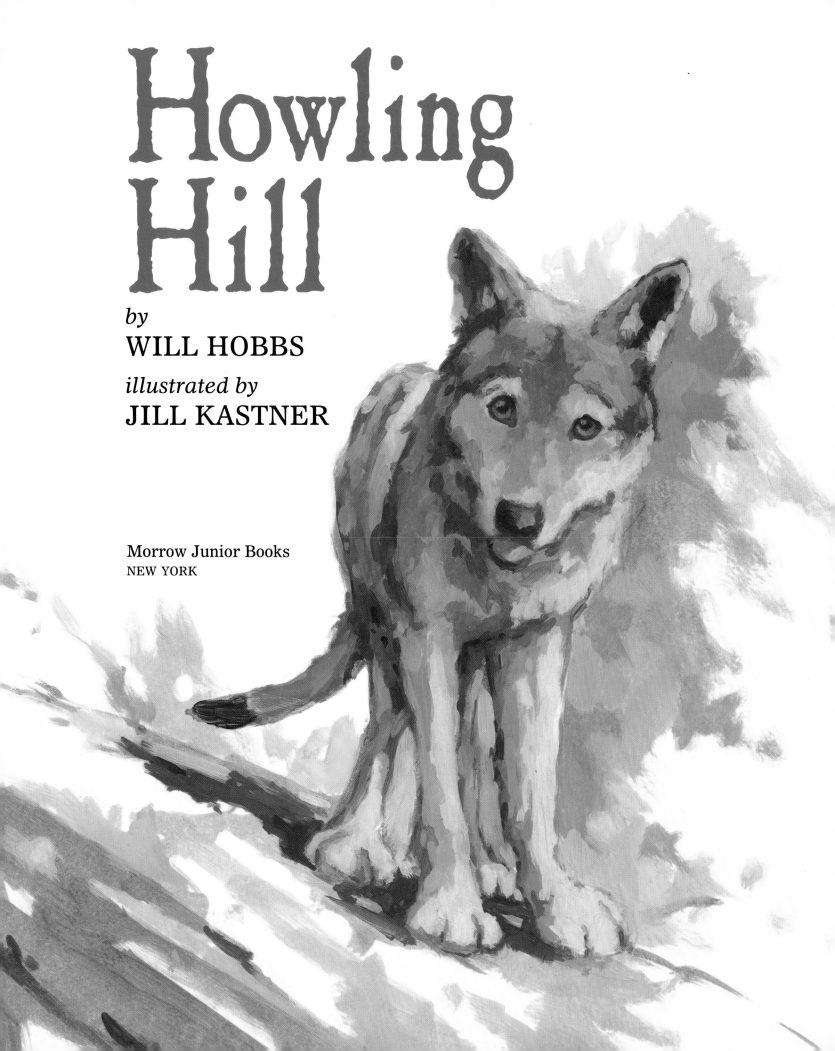

In the far, far north, deep in the wilds, a wolf pup named Hanni stepped carefully through the puddles of hot, stinky water. She was following her family to the top of Howling Hill, where the steaming water bubbled out of the ground. It was their favorite place to howl.

Her father started howling first, and then everyone else joined in, even her brothers and sisters. But when Hanni tried to howl, all that came out were little barks and yips. No matter how hard she tried to break into a howl, the sound just wouldn't come out. Hanni was so disappointed. She wanted more than anything to join in the song of her family.

"Don't worry," her mother reassured her. "It's inside of you, Hanni, somewhere deep inside."

Hanni's family came down from Howling Hill and began to run, twisting and leaping among the falling leaves. Hanni loved to run and play with her family. They ran on and on, over the hills and down into the valleys, until they came to a river. Her father told her that she was named after this river, the great Nahanni.

In her happiness, Hanni was dancing on a log with her brothers and sisters. Suddenly she turned around and discovered that she was the only one left on the log—and the log was moving. She was floating down the river, away from the shore and away from her family!

Hanni didn't know what to do. She ran back and forth on the log as her family raced after her along the shore, trying to keep up. Should she jump into the river? She had never been in the river before, and the current was so fast.

Hanni clung tight to the log as it swept under the cliffs and around the bend. She looked back upstream, only to find that her family had disappeared.

For the first time in her life, Hanni was alone. She cried and she whined and she whimpered, but her cries were lost in the wilderness.

All day and all night she floated on, among hissing cakes of ice. The next day, from downstream, came a mighty sound like thunder. As she floated closer, the sound grew into a terrible roar. Hanni knew she had to get to shore. She summoned all her courage and leaped into the river.

To her surprise, her legs knew how to swim. She paddled swiftly in the icy water, keeping her face up. The shore was so far away!

Hanni swam until she thought she couldn't swim any longer, and then she swam some more. She swam until she dragged herself onto the shore.

Hanni soon discovered what was making all the noise. She was looking at the great falls of the Nahanni.

The roar of the mighty waterfall scared her. She felt very small and very, very alone. Raising her head, Hanni tried to howl, but all that came out was a little "Yip, yip, yip."

Hanni crept into the forest to find a place to hide. Among the roots of a cottonwood tree, she curled up in a ball and let the last golden leaves fall on her until they almost covered her up.

The next day, in her lonely searching, Hanni saw a dark hole in the mountainside that reminded her of the den, far away, where she was born. She tiptoed inside. "Hello," Hanni called softly. "Is anybody in here?"

"Just someone trying to get to sleep," a deep voice replied.

Hanni took a few cautious steps forward. Now she could see who was in the den. It was a bear, enormous and fat. "I didn't mean to wake you," Hanni apologized.

The bear sighed. "Oh, I was just tossing and turning anyway. I've been trying to get to sleep for a week. Every year I have the same problem."

"I have a problem too," Hanni said. "I'm a long way from home, and I'm really, really lost."

"I know exactly where you're from," the bear told her.

"You do?"

"I can smell it on your fur. It's that place where the hot, smelly water bubbles out of the top of a hill."

Hanni was amazed. "That's right," she said. "That's Howling Hill! Can you take me there?"

The bear thought long and hard. "Maybe I can, little wolf," he answered at last. "I have another den closer to where you live. I slept there last winter. By the time we get there, I'm bound to be sleepy."

The next morning it wasn't so easy to leave the den. The entrance was blocked by something damp and white. The big bear pushed his way out into the open, with Hanni following. Overnight the world had changed completely. "What is it?" Hanni asked, bewildered.

"Snow," the bear replied.

She took a bite of it. The snow tasted good, Hanni thought, but as she tried to follow the bear, she found that walking in it was difficult. Then she realized she could leap from one of the bear's tracks to the next, and that made it easier to keep up.

Every day it got colder, so much colder. One day the big bear left the forest and walked right out onto the river. When Hanni followed, she discovered that the river had turned to ice!

As they walked up the frozen river, Hanni noticed that the bear was starting to yawn, a little at first and then all the time. "I'm getting so sleepy," he said as he trudged along. "So very sleepy."

A little while later, the bear fell asleep standing up. He even started to snore.

Hanni barked and barked, but she couldn't wake him up. Then she stood on her hind legs and tugged on his fur with all her might.

Finally the bear's weary eyelids opened. "Oh," he said, blinking and looking all around. "This is where we have to leave the river."

Yawning, he led her up the creeks and over the hills. At last, at a place known only to him, the bear began to scratch in a snowbank. But he was much too tired to dig.

Hanni dug for him. She dug furiously, until she uncovered the entrance to his old den.

Hanni knew the bear couldn't stay awake more than a few moments longer. "Tell me, before you go inside. How will I ever find Howling Hill?"

With a tremendous yawn, the bear said, "I can smell the stinky water from here. Just follow your nose. Good luck, little wolf!"

With that, the bear disappeared into his den, and Hanni found herself alone once more.

There was nothing left to do but wrinkle her nose and sniff the wind. Hanni thought she could smell the stinky water, very faintly.

She set out bravely but soon lost the scent.

She tried again, and this time her nose was more sure of itself. She kept going.

At last Hanni caught sight of a peculiar cloud rising into the sky. It was Howling Hill! She started to climb, sure that her family would be waiting at the top. The warm water felt good running over her tired paws.

But when she reached the top, no one was there. Hanni looked in every direction. All she could see was the endless forest. She tried to howl, but all that came out were the same little barks and yips, not the singing howl that would carry across the wilderness to her family.

Exhausted and all out of hope, Hanni lay down to rest. As darkness fell, the northern lights cast their ghostly shimmering dance across the sky.

When she thought of her brothers and sisters, her parents, her aunts and her uncles, Hanni's loneliness came pouring out. She stood up, lifted her head, and began to howl. From deep inside, her howl came out. She howled pure and loud, long and lonely. Hanni howled and howled again.

Her voice carried far across the frozen stillness. Far away, where her family had bedded down for the night, her mother and her father perked up their ears. "It's Hanni!" they cried.

By dawn she could see them coming, all of them, leaping and bounding their way up Howling Hill. Her brothers and sisters licked her face and leaped for joy. They were all together again.

Then they began to howl, first her father, then her mother, then all the rest. And this time Hanni joined in. She lifted her head and howled magnificently. From deep inside, her song came pouring out. At last Hanni was adding her voice to the song of her family.

To Katie and Lily, my youngest nieces
—W.H.

For Will and Jean
—J.K.

Oil paints were used for the full-color illustrations. The text type is 14-point Dutch 811.

Text copyright © 1998 by Will Hobbs. Illustrations copyright © 1998 by Jill Kastner.

Published by Morrow Junior Books, a division of William Morrow and Company, Inc., 1350 Avenue of the Americas, New York, NY 10019
www.williammorrow.com

Printed in Singapore at Tien Wah Press.

10 9 8 7 6 5 4 3

Library of Congress Cataloging-in-Publication Data
Hobbs, Will.
Howling Hill/by Will Hobbs; illustrated by Jill Kastner.
p. cm.
Summary: While separated from her family in the wilderness area along the Nahanni River,
a wolf pup discovers that she can express her loneliness in a long, loud howl.
ISBN 0-688-15429-8 (trade)—ISBN 0-688-15430-1 (library)
[1. Wolves—Fiction. 2. Wilderness areas—Fiction.] I. Kastner, Jill, ill. II. Title. PZ7.H6524Ho 1998 [E]—dc21 97-32915 CIP AC

QUAKERTOWN COMMUNITY SCHOOL DISTRICT